TITCH AND DAISY

Pat Hutchins

TITCH AND

Harcourt

Orlando   Boston   Dallas   Chicago   San Diego

Visit *The Learning Site!*
www.harcourtschool.com

DAISY

This edition is published by special arrangement with Greenwillow Books, a division of William Morrow & Company, Inc.

Grateful acknowledgment is made to Greenwillow Books, a division of William Morrow & Company, Inc. for permission to reprint *Titch and Daisy* by Pat Hutchins. Copyright © 1996 by Pat Hutchins.

Printed in the United States of America

ISBN 0-15-313404-6

3 4 5 6 7 8 9 10 179 02 01 00

For Barbara and Henning
to read to their grandchildren

Titch didn't want to go
to the party.
"You'll make new friends,"
said Mother, "and Daisy
will be there."

Titch looked for Daisy, but
Daisy wasn't there.
"Hello," said the other children.
"Come and play with us!"
But Titch didn't want to play
if Daisy wasn't there.

He hid behind the door and
watched them playing all his
favorite games.
He wished Daisy were there.

"Come and dance with us!"
said the other children.
But Titch didn't want to dance
if Daisy wasn't there.

So he crept behind the sofa
and watched them dancing
all his favorite dances.
He wished Daisy were there.

"Come and sing with us!" said
the other children.
But Titch didn't want to sing
if Daisy wasn't there.

So he peeped out of the cupboard and listened to them singing all his favorite songs. He wished Daisy were there.

"Come and eat with us!" said
the other children.
But Titch didn't want to eat
if Daisy wasn't there.

He crawled under the table,
which was covered with all his
favorite things to eat.
He wished Daisy were there.

And she was.

"I hid under the table when I
couldn't find you," said Daisy.
"I kept wishing you were here."

"PLEASE come and eat with us,"
said the other children.
And Titch and Daisy did.

They ate all their favorite food.

And they danced,
and sang
all their favorite songs,

and played all their
favorite games,

and made lots of new friends.